The Talon

Volume 3
Spring 2019

The Pink Sprinkles Edition

*Special thanks to
Chris Murphy, Chris Flavin, and Write Club
for their help with and support of The Talon*

Ode to Tequila

Oh tequila, tequila! Evil, cruel tequila.
"I've been personally victimized by tequila;
the first time I ever drank it was the last time," Bailey replied.

Oh tequila, tequila! Sweet, victimless tequila.
"We've had a come-to-Jesus moment, tequila
and I," Missy sighed.

Oh bourbon, oh bourbon! Sinful, liquid, bourbon.
"I like tequila just fine, but bourbon?
Thirty years ago, I had a fight with bourbon and it won," Charlie
    professed.

Oh tequila, tequila! Devious, fibber tequila.
"I tried it once and it lied. Tequila,
I still can't dance," Emily denied.

Oh tequila, tequila! Wretched, awful tequila.
"I don't like tequila.
My body rejected it, I threw up in the sink," Ashlea cried.

Oh bourbon, oh bourbon! Stinky, horrid bourbon.
"I avoid it. The last time I had bourbon,
I shit in my cat's litter box," a customer confessed.

Oh tequila, tequila! Low-priced, offensive tequila.
"If it's not cheap, I like tequila;
but I don't like that one. I have better taste," Mari simplified.

Oh tequila, tequila. Repugnant, undignified tequila.
"I like silver tequila.
I don't like to drink it now," Michael tried.

Oh alcohol, alcohol! You're a deceitful beast.
"I've shared other's confessions,
yet I'll share none of mine," I write from my desk.

Year Walk

A bitter wind blew through the narrow streets of Honeysuckle, a small Missouri town hidden deep in the Ozarks, and Alice knew that it was her grandmother who called on those frosted iron clouds that followed after the cold snap. She had seen it before, her grandmother call on winds or ask for them to leave, the offerings of tobacco and drink and other vices in exchange for little charms when the townsfolk needed a bit of luck. The offerings came most often from the elders or those that Alice's grandmother proclaimed "know to fear both God and those we brought here with us."

"Who are those we brought here, Mormor?" Alice often asked. Alice never got a clear answer from her grandmother. The woman would ramble about strange creatures until her English developed into low Swedish ramblings, spit a few times behind her left shoulder, and clasp her hands in prayer that always beseeched God as the Allsmäktig. Alice's mother told her not to ask those sorts of questions unless it was very important.

Mormor's dark clouds rolled in the night after Christmas and for five days it snowed off and on until the streets had been forgotten under white blankets of ice.

"Is Mormor angry at the town, Mom?" Alice asked. She looked out of one of the windows, exhaled large breaths on the glass to draw bored smiles that looked at toward the town, and rolled onto her back on the bar window sofa to see the smile that she drew upside down.

"No, sweetie, Mormor ain't angry at the town," Elsa said. "Well, maybe she's mad at Mister Holliday next door, but you know she'd rather cuss and spit at him all day than have him all boarded up inside."

Alice sighed. "Then why is she makin' it snow so long?"

Alice's mother was silent for a moment, the girl left alone with faded smiles on the window turned upside down, until that blonde curly-headed woman knelt down by her daughter at the window seat. Her full lips parted as she smiled wide and stroked

Alice's golden hair, and Alice's emerald eyes stared up at her mother, and for a moment Alice noticed the pain behind her eyes she tried to hide.

"Alice, listen now, we're gonna have some company coming soon," she said. "A gentleman, who um…" Alice's chest tightened as her mother's eyes darted into the air above them. "Who looks out for people like us. He just asks we do him and his friends a few favors from time to time."

Alice nodded. She was used to her grandmother and mother taking care of the people of Honeysuckle, and there were times when Elsa and Alice's Mormor asked her to go outside or stay in her room to keep her away from certain people. But a child's mind is often filled with morbid curiosities and inhuman bravery that many adults lose, so Alice had seen those ethereal green flames and dead dim lights of her family's secrets that would one day be passed to her.

"Do you want me up in my room then?" she asked.

"No, Alice, I have to ask you for a favor." Her mother exhaled. "I don't want to ask you to do this…Lord Almighty, if only I could keep you away from all this for a little longer."

Alice sat up with a push from her pointy elbows and her heart raced enough that her chest visibly leapt out with every beat of her heart, her eyes widening. "What do you need me to do?"

⟡⟡

A loud knock came from the front door as Alice sat in the kitchen with Mormor. Her grandmother sprinkled an oil on her forehead that smelled of walnuts and wolfsbane, her voice low as she murmured what Alice assumed was either a spell or prayer in Swedish. From the kitchen, she heard a new voice that echoed along with her mother from the living room, and Mormor paused as she bent forward and lightly kissed Alice once on the lips. Alice blinked, then Mormor stood up and walked behind her with hands that squeezed her shoulders tight when the two bodies approached.

The first was a tall man with thick brown hair that was cut short and parted to the right, olive-toned skin, and a bit of stubble that had grown after a day without a shave. His lean body hidden beneath a form-fitting overcoat that draped a little past his knees,

4

and upon seeing Alice a warm smile spread across his face that was returned with a cold glare from Mormor.

The man cleared his throat into a clenched fist as his brow furrowed and eyes darted away from the elder, but soon he took a step toward Alice and knelt down to speak with her at eye level in her chair.

"You must be Alice," he said. "It's nice to meet you."

"Nice to meet you, Mister…"

"Eli." Eli's smile spread from ear to ear, his eyes wrinkled, and he offered Alice his hand.

"Nice to meet you, Mister Eli," she said. Alice took Eli's hand and shook it once before they pulled apart and the man nodded.

"How old are you, Alice?" Eli asked.

"Twelve."

Eli nodded and his warm smile melted away as he stood back up and reached into his coat pocket to remove a letter sealed with red wax. "Alice, do you know what you're doing tonight?"

Alice's mother chimed in, "We've told her. She knows what she's doing, my mother has her prepped."

"Miss Olsson, I want to hear her say it," Eli said. His eyes darted only briefly at Alice's mother, then he returned his piercing eyes back at Alice.

"Year Walk, I'll be locked in a dark room all day and when it's midnight I'll head to the church," Alice said.

Eli nodded. "You'll see things, Alice, your world will change after tonight." He handed Alice the envelope and patted the back of her hands when they grasped at the paper. "Give this letter to the Kirk Grim when you see it."

Alice's eyes looked up to make contact with Eli's own only to notice that even though he looked back at her, his eyes saw past the girl as he was lost in thought. He gulped and sighed once and let go of Alice's hand to leave as Alice's mother escorted him out of the kitchen.

"Who is that, Mormor?"

"En Jägare," Her grandmother said. The elder tightened her grasp on her granddaughter's shoulders and spat over her own left shoulder.

⤫⤬

Alice had been placed in an empty room without light, the heat turned off, and had gone without food for over fifteen hours. Each hour crawled away from her with a dreadful boredom and hunger that tempted her to escape the frigid room. But had she done that the ritual would have been ruined, and this was just another step closer to being like her mother and Mormor. And for that reason, she endured the pains of an empty stomach, the cold bite of the air, and the lull of sleep in the darkness.

She shook and breathed fogged breaths into her open palms and curled into her coat as best she could, but the cold was the least of her concerns as her mind raced with the dreadful warning her Mormor gave her of those creatures that had been brought here by those that know to fear God. And though this knowledge excited her, there was dread that filled her being to know that just beyond the safe walls of her home there have always been boogeymen, and, more awful still, many of these boogeymen followed the settlers from the old world into the new world generations ago.

Midnight struck, an old oak grandfather clock chimed down the hall, and Alice lifted her face from her knees and she stood up. She approached the door and placed her hand on the knob, and for a moment she hesitated. Perhaps sleep was better than going for walk out into the elements. She could just head to her room, curl up in her covers, and fall asleep to pretend the next day that she learned nothing of her family's reality. She could be a normal child again.

She twisted the knob and the door opened up to the moonlit darkness of the hallway. The house was silent. This was her chance, her mother wouldn't blame her if she changed her mind at the last second. All she had to do was turn right down the hall and her room would offer sanctuary from the eldritch truth. She patted her coat pocket and felt the letter that was stuffed near her breast and before she knew it she turned left down the hallway.

She went from the living room then out the front door only to be smacked by a wall of air that froze in her lungs with each breath and her boots ankle deep in a snowdrift. The town of Honeysuckle was darkened by the apex of night, the shadows tamped by the soft sparkle of moonlight against the fresh fallen snow, but in the distance, the wooded Ozark hills that peered over the town like giants had millions of glowing eyes within that stared down at the streets.

Every so often Alice's breath would halt as she held the air in her lungs, when she swore that some of those eyes stared right at her before they blinked and were gone. The darker portions of the streets hid the speakers of soft whisperers that openly gossipped about the young girl; the numerous voices giggled and jeered at Alice from the darkened shadows of alleyways and within the gardens of many of the homes she passed. But soon the millions of eyes faded away and the whispers became inaudible as soft breezes blown by the hills drowned out all other noise.

The silence of the voices and the disappearance of the eyes gave Alice the courage to keep walking down the road, but within the corner of her eye always stood the figure of a tall man that passed between the trees just beyond. In her mind, he appeared old, green, tall and thick as an oak, and had a beard of moss and fallen leaves. Alice stopped in her tracks every few feet just to catch a glimpse of that wildman, but when her eyes darted to the last spot she had seen the blur of movement there was nothing but the darkness between the trees and the deafening whistle of winter's wind.

This continued for blocks as Alice walked toward the New Jerusalem Church, but often she wasn't fast enough to catch the man between the trees who followed her close.

"He's watching you," a tiny voice rang. Alice spun in place on her heels to catch a glimpse of whatever spoke to her from behind. A small winged creature no bigger than a hummingbird hovered just a foot in front of her face.

"Who is?" Alice's question almost froze in her throat. She had heard from her mother that a number of fairies lived in these parts, but to see a pixie up close caused the air in her lungs to halt for a brief moment.

"He is the king of the forest," another tiny voice sang. Alice's head turned as more of these tiny winged elves gathered around her. A faint blue and purple glow beamed off their bodies, much like fireflies.

"He is a god," another rebutted.

Alice stared at the creatures and moved backward, the snow crunching under her foot. And the group of fairies all buzzed around her.

"Come and see him!"

"Yes! He loves to meet little witches!"

"Follow us, Alice."

Alice shook her head, her emerald eyes wide as they darted between each of the tiny creatures whose group continued to grow in size.

"How do you know my name?" The little witch backed away from the creatures.

"Where are you going, Alice?"

She didn't answer. The girl turned around on her heel once more and trudged through snow as fast as her little legs could allow. The pixies flew past her ears like large mosquitoes, their dragonfly wings buzzing, unlike any bug she had ever heard before.

"The river! She's headed toward the river!"

"Alice, you mustn't go toward the river!"

A sharp yelp escaped Alice's lips as she ran. Her hands slapped hard against her red ears—numbed by the cold. Her breath became ragged, fear and exhaust, but she pushed forward with her eyes shut tight.

"Let her go!"

"Yes, let her go!"

The fairies all agreed, blinked their purple-hued blue light one last time, and vanished just as they had appeared. Alice continued to run forward with eyes closed until there were no more unearthly flashes that glimmered past her eyelids. She slowed down, opened her eyes, and removed her hands from her ears. Alice stood in place and stared all around here but she was alone.

Alice patted the letter in her coat breast pocket and walked toward the church just beyond the river that cut through the small town.

The covered bridge came into view just beyond a small iced slope, and the playing of a guitar filled the air and broke that silence. It was welcome, and the pluck of the strings hummed in her ear and her heart eased, and the voice of the man that sang along with it was low and smooth. Alice's mind clouded as his words filled her head and filled her with a pleasure she had never felt before.

The Singer stood there on the frozen river, his body built strong, his arms like tree trunks that swelled beyond the rolled-up cuffs of his white button up. Black suspenders roped past his chest and held up his slick black pants. His features were strong but clean, his face made of rock that had been chiseled by gentle waters, and his voice placed the image of a babbling brook in Alice.

> *As I went down in the river to pray*
> *Studying about that good ol' way*
> *And who shall wear the starry crown?*
> *Good Lord show me the way*

His voice rang out toward her and his eyes flashed when Alice drew closer. Each step she took, her head grew cloudier and she couldn't think of anything except for The Singer, and he smiled a large set of white teeth that glimmered in the light of the moon like the ice around him. Alice focused only on that man. Her feet moved further away from the road to the covered bridge and then slid carefully as she stepped onto the ice.

> *O sisters let's go down*
> *Let's go down, come on down*
> *O sisters let's go down*
> *Down in the river to pray!*

Alice's feet carried her closer to The Singer as he smiled wide and continued to play that guitar. That silver bolo tie around his neck swayed and she now saw the engraved image of ten-pointer buck skull. The ice below her cracked and strained from the girl's weight and as she reached out her hand to touch The Singer. The Singer stopped playing that guitar for a moment only to sing and reached his hand to touch Alice's own, and when he had the ice gave out and she plunged into the dark swirling chaos below. Too cold to swim so she sank; too dark to see so she was blind.

⊷⊷

Alice coughed and her gut wrenched as she turned her head and vomited water. Her head pounded hard and tears welled up in her

9

eyes. The walk had proven too much for the girl, and when she opened her eyes she stared up into the sky. The stars moved and flew through the air in a background of purple, blues, and black more active than before.

"Your grandmother is a smart woman," a voice said. "I smelled the walnuts and wolfsbane and found you just as the nøkk tried to drag you under."

Alice picked herself up. Her body shivered and her lips were blue. She was now on the other side of the river where the church was, and out on the frozen river, The Singer was gone. What took his place was a drenched head with damp hair that clumped on its scalp and white dead eyes that peered over at her where she had fallen through the ice. Alice's heart raced. The fear of those dead eyes burned her blood and jolted her with enough warmth to breathe once more.

"Don't stare too long," the voice said. "I doubt he's happy he just lost his dinner."

Alice spun on her heel toward the voice only see a large black dog sitting in the snow with its head tilted to the side. She looked past the dog and at the church and the woods around it.

"Wh-who said that?" she asked.

"Don't act like you don't see me, it's rude," the black dog said. Alice's eyes widened and the dog got back on all fours and padded toward the church.

"I'm sorry," Alice said. Her brow furrowed as she stood there in place. The Year Walk had taken much of her strength and tested her nerves beyond any normal child's breaking point, but if she was to be as powerful as her Mormor or her mother she knew she would have to endure.

"It's alright," the dog said. He turned his head to look at the girl and used his tail to signal for her to follow. "Come on now, you'll catch yourself a death in your sorry state. Let's get you into the church to warm up and finish your walk."

Alice prodded forward in short bursts of speed to catch up to the dog and nodded her head. She was wary to trust anything as it was now, but she knew the dog was right—if she stayed outside the church the cold would kill her now.

"Who are you?" Alice asked, now beside the dog, as they got to the front doors of the New Jerusalem Church.

"The church grim, kirk grim, your grandmother would say Kirkonväki, but honestly I never spoke Swedish that well so you can just call me Kirk if you want." The church grim sat down on his hind legs and stared up at Alice as she, in turn, looked down at him and shivered. A few seconds of silence washed over the two until the dog shifted his weight and cleared his throat.

"I, um, I can't open the doors for you until you finish the walk, so if you could…"

"Oh, sorry…" Alice stumped backward as she began to walk around the church but stopped herself as she faced the other direction now.

"Counterclockwise."

"Right, sorry."

Alice circled the church three times counterclockwise and approached the doors of the church to press her lips to the keyhole and blow. The doors swung open and the dog walked into the church and the doors closed as Alice took a few steps inside. She walked to one of the pews and sat down, and the dog came back with a few blankets in his mouth to hand to Alice.

"Get out of those wet clothes, wrap yourself up, and lie on the ground so I can curl up next to you," Kirk said.

"But what about the visions?" Alice asked. She pulled the letter out from her pocket when she remembered and handed the soggy bit of paper to the dog. "A man named Eli wanted me to give you this."

The church grim took the letter and shook his head some until the wet envelope tore open and then laid the letter on the floor to read. Alice stared at the dog as she undressed from her wet clothes and began to wrap herself up in the blankets.

"Ah, I see," Kirk said. "You are their new seer, yes, it makes sense now why it was you that showed up and not your mother or grandmother."

"What do you mean?"

"Your grandmother and mother can't make this walk anymore, it will have to be you from now on," the church grim said.

"I don't understand," Alice said.

"You didn't happen to notice a large green man hiding in the trees, did you?"

Alice nodded.

"He's an old forest spirit, fancies himself a god, so whenever someone like you hedge witches go for too many Year Walks he eventually confronts you. If you're not able to stand up against him he won't allow you to do it anymore.

Alice yawned as her eyelids went heavy. She shivered and took a gulp of air as she hugged her covers close. The church grim padded close to her and curled up next to her.

"Lie down, child, sleep and you will be given your visions."

∽◌∾

The church was full of people that Alice had never seen before, many of whom wore strange masks of clay shaped into faces fixed into their final moments of death. There she sat in the back pew of the church next to her mother and her Mormor. Her Mormor's head rested in the lap of her daughter, Elsa. She was unmoving and cold yet peaceful. Tears ran down Elsa's face as she brushed her mother's grey hair and poor Alice couldn't act—she could only watch.

A loud yell drew Alice's eyes to the front of the of the church and a few of the masked people stood up from their pews and apporached those without masks. With guns in hand, the masked men and women fired on those without clay faces and the those without masks fought back with claws and biting. A massacre ensued and one by one people from both ends of the conflict began to sit back down in the pews and act as if nothing had happened, except for a maskless woman. She was covered in blood as she straddled a man's body with his throat in her mouth and with a little girl that sat next to her. In the opposite corner, a masked man held tight to the figures of an adult woman and young girl both slumped over in his arms.

The masked weeper stood up as he dropped the bodies of the girls and approached the wild woman who still drank deep the blood of her recent kill. The masked man pulled a gun and fired into the head of the wild woman and she fell over dead. The man reached up and pulled off his mask to reveal the face of Eli, the man that sent Alice on her Year Walk. He reached over and grabbed the little girl that now sat alone and walked her over to the bodies of the dead girls he held onto earlier. He removed the mask from the dead younger girl, her features similar to his own, and tried to fit the mask onto the girl he had taken.

❧❧

Alice's mother found her that morning wrapped up in blankets and her body warm and alive. Both their eyes welled up in tears and they shared a laugh between each other for a moment at the joy of being together, but for Alice, the laughs soon developed into wails and her body shook between shortened cut-off breaths as she held on tight to her mother's warm body. The glowing eyes in the mountains, the whispers, the tall wildman that followed her, and worse the dead eyes of The Singer flashed into her mind once more.

These things, all these things that her mother had protected her from, lived so close yet unseen within their small town hidden in the Ozarks. Her mother held her tight and rocked her back and cradled her in her arms. Tears rushed down her face and splashed onto Alice. How could she have done this to her own daughter, how could she reveal the horrors of this world to her at such a young age? The guilt riddled her brain and broke her heart.

The doors swung open and Eli walked into the church and over to the daughter and mother, but he didn't dare break up the moment between them. He wasn't heartless, guilt washed over him as well, and he suffered his own self-inflicted rage silently in the pew just across from the two. Hunters can often be as bad as the monsters they track. Two hours passed in that church until Alice had calmed down and Eli picked himself up and knelt down to address Alice.

"Alice, did you give the church grim the letter?" he asked.
She nodded.
"Did you see visions?"
Alice nodded.
"What did you see, sweetie?"
Alice's brow furrowed and she shook her head as she crossed her arms and curled up in those blankets that draped over her.
"Eli, I'm sorry."

13

Spring

A light dusting of frost
glitters in the golden morning:
tiny diamonds resting on amber earth.

Tufts of new growth bloom:
emerald and jade,
ruby and cerulean.

Flowers peek into the brilliance,
tender blossoms of
amethyst and citrine.

Birdsong echoes from sapphire breasts
as peridot and coral buds
begin to emerge amongst the trees.

Unspoken promises
of rebirth and renewal burst
from snowy slumber.

Up With the Sun

Up with the Sun,
O Apollo, O Ra,
Hashem Tzevaot,
Or gravity, all!

Up with the Sun,
Spirit of the sky, O Surya great.
Shine on us all
Your wisdom today!

Guide us in truth,
In love, and in light.
Give us this day
To aid in our sight!

An Abject Abstract

What if the hummingbird
Could open its mouth
And penguins of all shapes
Could travel South

What if it was gold
That killed the undead
Would silver become
Corrupt in its stead

Perhaps a flying pig
Is all that stands between
Hope and Wishing
On stars that gleam

Perhaps light cannot be
Exceeded because time
Is a dimension barred
From Eve's crime

According to
Factual falsification
"Anything is possible"
Is an implication

Twoworlds

Mystic Indian

Fasting today
Waiting for a vision
Doing a sweat today
Grass is green
Rivers flow
Nature sings to me
Woman she calls to me
Day is over—rest
Night falls—comes darkness

Mystified Indian

Hungry, no commods in fridge
No shows—TV repairman's late
Sweating today—darn air conditioner broke again
Gotta mow the darn yard again
Working today and rain never stops
So many dogs barking and crows a-kaw-ing
Dang cell phone—wife is calling again
Another long day at work
Oh shoot, another power outage

On Turkey Mountain

The philosophy of heart,
With hopeful and in-tune energy,
Runs through each and ev'ry tree.
This heart is the heart of the cosmos…
The silence.
The ethos.

The ethos of this place is peace.
A peace made of negligence…
A long-foregone peace.

I steal away, and hope
To not leave again
That neglected peace.
That hope of nature.

Mr. Melvin Quit Today

I moved to Podunk, Oklahoma with my dad halfway through the eighth grade. Podunk was a little different than what I was used to. It was a small town where everyone had known everyone all the way back to kindergarten, and their parents all went to school together when they were younger, and their parents' parents did the same. It seemed like school was something people did here out of habit, more or less.

The words "Podunk Pirates" were written on the outside of the school in chipping purple paint and the grass around the building was overgrown. "Well, it's not as nice at your old school, but you'll get used to it bud," said my dad. "I guess I don't really have a choice," I said as I hopped out of the truck. I decided I would just lay low, finish out the year, and pray Podunk High School was a little bit nicer. "I'm sorry. You'll just have to make the most of it. Good luck, Zach, and have a nice day, little man," he said before driving off.

I walked into the office and met Miss Brown, the secretary. She asked me my name and told me to have a seat, then clacked at an old computer for a while without looking up. I was trying to figure out how someone's hair could possibly get so unruly and wondered if she even owned a brush. Then I remembered, I didn't brush my hair this morning either and I figured I'd fit right in here. She handed me my schedule and told me where my locker was. My first class of the day was science with a guy named Mr. Melvin, but it was already half over. I told her I didn't want to interrupt or cause a scene, but she insisted I go before I ended up even later. As I was walking out the door, Mrs. Brown stopped me and said, "Mr. Melvin's a little strange, but some of the kids here really like him."

I stood outside the classroom and put my ear up to the door and caught the middle of a lecture about photosynthesis. I knocked a couple times and the voice from inside stopped talking. I stood there silently for what felt like an abnormal amount of time before the voice finally called from within, "What's the password?"

I figured he was joking, so I walked inside without saying anything. Any normal person probably would have just let it go, but I was wrong for assuming Mr. Melvin was a normal person. A wiry old man with long white hair and John Lennon glasses stood in front of me looking shocked. "You couldn't even try to guess a password?" he asked.

"Wait, what?" I said, and the class snickered. I felt twenty pairs of eyes watching me melt into the floor. "You could have at least guessed some common ones," said Mr. Melvin. "Personally, I'd probably start with 123456, qwerty, or even just password in all lowercase." I had no idea what was going on, but my plan to lay low on my first day was going up in flames thanks to John Lennon's ghost. "What's your name?" he asked.

"Zach Martin," I said.

"Welcome to Podunk, Zach. Just have a seat at one either of those empty desks and pray it doesn't break when you put your weight on it. I promise that's not a quip about your weight. Those things really do break all the time. Also, I'm sorry, but we'll have to properly introduce you tomorrow if you make it to class on time. For now, it's time to learn," said Mr. Melvin. He clapped his hands and began again before I finished sitting down. I steered clear of the middle desk and made my way to one on the side while avoiding eye contact with every soul in the room. Mr. Melvin continued talking about plants as if he hadn't just dug my grave and buried me in it. Beside me was a huge bookshelf that took up the whole wall. It was full of books, toys, and knick-knacks. The other wall had a couple of windows and a poster with the Periodic Table. Up front was a wall-length chalkboard Mr. Melvin had filled with drawings and words relating to photosynthesis. In the corner by the door stood a tall fedora-wearing plastic skeleton he'd named Al Cabone. Mr. Melvin liked to say that Al could teach us not only about the bones in the body, but also what might happen if we resorted to organized crime later in life. Hell, I knew it couldn't be worse than Mr. Melvin's class.

At lunch, a girl named Morgan Fairchild asked me to trade some of my chicken nuggets for her roll. I obviously got the bad end of that deal, but I was pretty desperate to make some friends, so I took her offer. Mr. Melvin sat at the end of the teacher's table and didn't seem to be very interested in chatting with the rest of them. He brought his own lunch and drank from a thermos.

"So, what's that guy's deal?" I asked. "Oh, don't worry about him," laughed Morgan. "He's just a grumpy old hippy. I think he's kind of funny though, if you can stay off his radar. To be honest, he's actually one of the better teachers here."

She wasn't wrong. History was taught by a burly guy who only went by Coach. Morgan said the old history teacher died, and they couldn't find a replacement, so they gave Coach an emergency certification, and he'd taught history, PE, and coached the football team ever since.

I'm not sure how he managed to get away with it, but it seemed like Coach always found a way to work a movie into his lectures, and it drove Morgan crazy. She was convinced he was robbing us all of our education, and she'd always complain in his class. She'd raise her hand and say, "*The Patriot* isn't an accurate portrayal of the Revolutionary War," or "*School House Rock* is way below our age range." I didn't really mind the break, to be honest. Head down and pray the high school was better. Also, I would never admit it to Morgan, but I was starting to find those songs pretty catchy.

Math was a little harder to stomach for me. The work wasn't super difficult, and Mrs. Mahaney thought the subject well, but I had to sit in the back by this kid named Gage Bohannan. Gage probably would have been a pretty cool guy if he EVER SHUT UP. I'm pretty sure Mrs. Mahaney moved him back there so even *she* wouldn't have to listen to him anymore. Sometimes she'd send him to the office, but they'd just keep him there for the rest of the hour, and he'd be right back the next day, so we all tried to just ignore him for as long as we could. Sometimes it was difficult, though. His favorite thing to do was to lean close to me and whisper my name over and over. He'd say, "Zach Martin, Zach Martin, Zach Martin." If I acknowledged him, he'd just launch a wet paper wad at me with a rubber band, so I tried to stay vigilant. One day I managed to ignore him for fifty whole minutes, but I guess that just irritated him more, so for the last ten minutes he thought of the clever idea of changing my name altogether, and thus, I would forever be dubbed, "Snatch Fartin, Snatch Fartin,

Snatch Fartin." Gage somehow ended up passing Mrs. Mahaney's class that year. I guess he was better at math than we all thought.

After a couple months, I started enjoying Mr. Melvin's class a little more. He mostly left me alone aside from randomly calling me to read out loud or answer a random question about the lesson. Sometimes he'd get distracted and tell us crazy stories about his life, like how he hitchhiked to Woodstock back in the day, or how his oldest son ran away to Alaska to become a fisherman. I always wondered what he was doing there in Podunk. We would all make up stories about where he came from. I liked to think he was the victim of some failed CIA brain experiments or something and he moved out to Podunk to go into hiding. Morgan just thought he did a bunch of acid as a kid and it finally caught up to him. Honestly though, her story wasn't as cool. Sometimes he'd trail off stare into space for a minute. He was definitely a little looney, but he did know a lot about science.

One of the people who made Podunk a little more hellish for everyone was Gage's best friend, Big Matt. He was one of the only people to ever get held back in Junior High at Podunk. He told everyone his dad decided to due to his poor performance in class, but the rumor was that Coach talked his dad into it, so he could play another year of Junior High Football. I didn't know if the extra classroom time helped Matt get any more intelligent, but the Podunk Pirates Junior High team had a winning season that year, and Big Matt was named MVP.

Mr. Melvin was one of the only teachers who would try to keep Matt and Gage in line. That still didn't stop them from being disruptive. Some days, when they were both feeling particularly rowdy, they would feed off each other's energy and every class would be littered with obscenities, spontaneous laughter, any other type of distraction they could come up with. Mr. Melvin tried to keep them apart, but sometimes even he got tired of fighting with them, and he would simply teach as if they weren't there.

One day, Big Matt came up with the idea to challenge Mr. Melvin to an arm wrestling competition. Every day for two weeks Matt and Gage would taunt him. Matt would say, "Come on Melvin. You scared of getting beat by an eighth grader?" One day during attendance, Big Matt popped off again, and Mr. Melvin finally snapped. "Alright, that's it," he yelled and started walking towards Matt. Pure terror filled Matt's eyes and the room got quiet. Everyone knew Big Matt was about meet death in the middle of our eighth grade science class, but suddenly Mr. Melvin turned a desk around and slammed his elbow down on it. The class roared, and we all turned our desks to face the middle. Even Morgan scooted her chair a little closer to get a better view. The two locked arms, and the class went wild. "What's the matter," asked Mr. Melvin, "you scared of getting beat by an old man?" Big Matt flashed a toothy grin and the two started.

Big Matt was straining to gain leverage, but Mr. Melvin held steady. The match roared on for several minutes, and Big Matt began to sweat. Slowly, Matt started to gain the upper hand, and for a moment it looked like Mr. Melvin was about to lose, but suddenly, Mr. Melvin said, "I'd love to do this all day, but I have a class to teach. I just wanted to see you sweat," and pulled Matt's hand up, then back down to the table. The class went wild and everyone stood applauding as the two shook hands. Big Matt laid his head on his desk and the class settled down as Mr. Melvin walked back up to the front and said, "The secret is to let your opponent do most of the work. He used all his energy trying beat me early on, so all I really had to do is hold steady and maintain, then strike when they're at their weakest. Now that that's settled, let's get back to work." For the rest of the hour, Mr. Melvin had the whole class's undivided attention aside from Big Matt, but even Gage Bohannan sat quietly until the bell rang.

Mr. Melvin was late to class the next day, and Big Matt wasn't there at all. The clock above the door read about ten minutes past time for class to begin. Whispers about what could happened with the two of them were floating through the classroom. Morgan looked over to me from her desk on the other side of the room and pointed at her cell phone. I took mine out and read her text under the desk: "Matt's sister said he came home crying, and that their dad came up to the school to complain, and he was PISSED" with the shoulder shrugging emoji at the end.

Gage stood up and walked to the front of the class and spoke in the most proper voice he could muster, "Good morning, everybody. My name is Mr. Bohannan. It looks like I will be subbing for Mr. Melvin today." Half the class laughed, and Morgan yelled, "Sit down dumbass." Gage stood up straighter and put his hand over his mouth. "Why, that's no way to talk to your teacher, young lady. Keep that up, and I'll give you an arm-wrestling match you'll never forget," he said, flexing his arm. More laugher. "Alright, settle down, settle down," said Gage. He walked over to skeleton Al Cabone and picked him up by the arms. "Today we're going to talk about Dem Bones, Dem Bones, and Al here is going to be an example of what happens here at Podunk to eighth-graders who challenge me in front of my class." That got them good. The class roared as Mr. Bohannan began to waltz with the skeleton.

Just then Mr. Melvin flew through the door, letting it slam behind him, and yelled, "Sit down and shut up." Gage jumped and ran to his seat. Al Cabone fell to the floor and his head rolled off. Mr. Melvin had a black eye, bloody nose, and a busted lip, and he held a large boombox on his shoulder. He walked quickly the front row of desks, causing Sarah Hudson to shield her face as if she were about to be hit. He walked past her to the empty desk behind her, sat the boombox on it, and lifted it over her head. Mr. Melvin brought the desk to the front of the room. He plugged the boombox into the wall under the chalkboard. He then picked up a piece of chalk and wrote the word KNOWLEDGE in big bold letters across the board, then sat in the desk facing the class.

The room was silent and still. Blood dripped from Mr. Melvin's nose onto the desk in front of him, and then his voice filled the quiet. "Albert Einstein once said, 'Teaching should be such that what is offered is perceived as a valuable gift and not as hard duty. Never regard study as duty but as the enviable opportunity to learn to know the liberating influence of beauty in the realm of the spirit for your own personal joy and to the profit of the community to which your later work belongs.'" A girl sniffled, a silent cry. "Teaching has become a *hard* duty for me. I try to prepare you for these tests and for college, but there is no joy here in this. Not for me. Not for you. The opposite of passion is apathy, and apathetic I have become. Not towards you, but toward the institution that has brought us here together in *Podunk*, Oklahoma. I have discovered that there is only one way out, and it's the same way we all got in up to this point here now." Mr. Melvin leaned back and pointed at the board. "That is your password. That is one thing they cannot take away, but you must be willing to accept it first. This is my gift to you." He leaned forward and pressed play on the stereo and turned up the volume. The greatest hits of Melanie began playing as he got up and walked out the door. We saw what we'd done to his song. His arm was finally pinned.

A Visitor to my Jail

In the elements I am left to stay, desolate as the toys.
Dead-locked doors don't budge to reveal me; it's but silent.
The ball, long lost in the overgrown grass, forgotten.
Daily, I command travelers from my jail.
But one day, this lone girl doesn't run.
She turns and coos to me with kind eyes.
A brave hand reaches out to stroke my face
and I let her. Her calm demeanor soothes
my lonely soul and I lay down at the fence
trying to get closer with small avail.
I suppress my bark and she strokes me
like the good dog I am. *Yes, good—*

Wolves Howl Softly

In our world in the dark there is light,
but in your world there is only night.
We're wolves; we stand on fours and twos;
your curiosity we ask you not to excuse.
We are not beasts or monsters to fear;
our sole intent is to be close and dear.
Journey with us into a non-modern age;
let us, we beg of you, be your sage.
We ask you to listen to our offense:
Early man thought us to be evil
and like heretics to serve the Devil.
Condemnation and execution was the law
and the inquisitors' hearts did not thaw.
Like the others, we became ammunition
for the chroniclers of superstition.
Better are we treated in modern days
unlike the foolish and olden ways.
For demonstration, I have brief examples:
A dog attacked Gevaudan, France in 1764
killing peasants and villagers by the score.
"The Beast of Gevaudan" they named him
and three years he feasted, limb by limb.
The king sent men to end his red pace
in the fall, and it became a snowy race.
Struck by a bullet, he fell into tranquility;
to call him "natural" they lacked morality.
Instead, they exclaimed, "A werewolf!"
In 1589, Peter Stubbe in a German village
spoke of 25 years of murder and pillage.
He changed into a wolf by aid of a belt,
an offer of the Devil's to whom he dearly felt.
If there was a belt, no one could find it;
it was assumed it was taken by a spirit.

Did they consider he may have been insane
or to have abandoned the Lord's lane?
Instead, they exclaimed, "A werewolf!"
Even in your fairy tales are you discriminating
to such a length you are incriminating.
Are you sure the Big, Bad Wolf in the wood
did not insist to Little Red Riding Hood
on carrying her basket for her
or to partake in her grandmother's supper?
To have "seen the wolf" in French slang
is to have lost one's virginity in a fling.
Could he not be the Little, Good Wolf?
You have listened to our offense.
Now we ask you to listen to our defense:
A pair of siblings were abandoned in the chill
and were found by a she-wolf on a hill.
By day, she fed them with her milk;
by night, she bedded them in her silk.
Romulus and Remus came of age,
and Romulus murdered Remus in a rage.
He set out to build a colossal home
and quickly fathered mighty Rome.
A she-wolf did the city have for its mother.
In the 12th century, Marie de France wrote a lay;
real or imaginary, no one is able to say.
Bisclavret is a baron married to a baroness,
a baroness anxious to learn the baron's stress.
She learns he changes into a wolf in the hour
the wolves begin to search and devour.
To his wolfen form he had no objection;
to his human self there is no question.
Real or imaginary, Bisclavret is a memory.
In 1662, old man Thiess sought to abide
we, the Benandanti, fought on Christ's side
the witches and Malandanti in hell
to ensure the harvests were kept well.
"The Hounds of God" he named our kind,
but the judges thought him of a senile mind.
He was not condemned or burnt away

but was sent with ten lashes on his way.
Thiess of Livonia fought a good fight.
As men treaded a strait in new land yonder
they discovered a cosmos of wonder.
They separated into tribes in every direction
and found themselves weavers of creation.
They became aware of the new land's king,
the coyote, whose howling did sing
a song of eternal joy thereafter,
and the land delivered Coyote the Trickster.
A better offer the first Americans could not ask.
Now that you have listened to our offense
and you have listened to our defense,
will you join us in equal harmony
as though in a bond of matrimony?
By ourselves we have survived in the light;
with us you can survive in the night.
Wolves howl softly...softly...
wolves howl softly...softly...
and you—will you howl softly, too?

Untitled

Hungry children laugh
from the sidewalk lining the street
where an old lady flips off
the cop who cut her off,
while weaving through traffic,
in a hurry to buy a drug from the teenager
just trying to feel alive because
her dad is drunk all the time,
and her mom is never home
because she works all day and night,
clearing plates from the tables,
where men sit in Armani suits,
while they make the decision to fire
the man who has worked for forty years,
who will now collect welfare for the first time,
from an office full
of people who hate working,
next door to a clinic,
where a woman stands,
speaking to a doctor,
who will influence her decision for
the baby growing inside her,
who will grow up
to take pictures on the beach,
where a girl in a wedding dress,
whose life was just beginning,
will be found dead
by a man who, distraught,
will buy a shotgun,
from a man who sits
in a ruined house,
where buyers come all day and night
to marvel at

the children across the street,
who still know how to laugh.

WM-FX195

We exist in different types of emotion. Common things, but different. Not to say humans don't all feel the same but descriptors for every emotion change radically from person to person. A love language is a personal interpretation of an atmosphere.

Love is when they stopped drinking before me so that I could pass out drunk 15 minutes later in their arms, love is the faint hum of the VHS player rewinding my favorite gore flick that they never would have watched if I hadn't asked them to. Love is when they remember my favorite candy flavor is peach and they try to get me peach-flavored soda for our anniversary (and love is when I don't hold it against them that they don't know all the Fanta flavors).

Love is the easiest emotion to define. You feel it as it happens, you can identify it both in and out of the moment. The one hardest to define is contentment. Contentment is what you identify when the moment has passed. You rarely find the time to go "yes, this is the moment where I'm alright", that always comes after.

For me it was in my first car, a 2000 Pontiac Grand Prix with no air conditioning and a broken gas gauge, but what it did have was a cassette player. When you drove in the summer you had to keep the windows down. I spent hours driving around with the wind blowing through the car with No Doubt's *Tragic Kingdom* playing along with R.E.M.'s *Automatic for the People* and *Green* albums. That car, which I dubbed the Mirth Mobile, was eventually technically stolen from me, but I kept the tapes.

While love is a specific language, and contentment spoken of in memory, the one emotion that changes the most from person to person is depression. Depression is felt in the moment, in memory, and what we do to cope with such emotions often ends up being permanently associated with it.

Depression is going days without eating enough. It's the whirl of my WM-FX195 cassette player as the tape reels spin and spin until Side A winds to an end, and from there it's either fuzzy static or a dial-up tone ending with an abrupt click and silence until you turn over the tape. It's watching *Pet Sematary* with dead eyes until I fall asleep, seeking out the grossest Italian horror films, it's drinking Jägermeister from the bottle because you can't be fucked to mix it with root beer. It's the pressure just beneath the skin and eyes that glaze over to form a mirror, reflecting what people want to see when they try and talk to you. Slow Moving, Hardly Speaking, Self-Isolating, Emotionally Draining and Verging on Self Destruction.

It's like living in a Dario Argento film, everything is dubbed so nothing matches up with what people say, there's paranoia, the sound is either too soft for you to hear or too loud for you to bear it, and you get used to living life in surrealism until it just stops. For me there are no beginning or end credits to these depressive episodes, as they take hold and release with no warning.

Depression is like love, it's based on memory and lived moments. Love is when they say they hope I get better.

Snowglobes

When you're standing on the edge of a bridge
All you can think about are snowglobes.
Ok, maybe that's not true for everyone
But as I stand on the edge of this bridge
I don't think about childhood memories
Encased in gold film and sun spots.
I think about how frigid that summer felt;
The summer you left.

I think about how small the rocks seem.
Like Creator, himself, took extra care in shaping them
To receive me and my lumbering burden.
I think if a car drives by fast enough,
It'll cause the snow to fall but I'm too
Scared to watch. Like, if I look down I'll lose
My nerve. If I look up, I'll find an excuse to
Stay.

Jagged, like my breath, my fingers grip the
Edge. I close my eyes as I count the months
It's been since I heard your laugh.
Brain says it doesn't count. Standing here
Does not count. I left my jacket.
I left my jacket and it doesn't count.

Mothers shouldn't have to plan their children's funerals.
So I stay and it doesn't count.

The Boardwalk

The moon hangs over the beach. It hangs heavy and low, as if it is struggling to avoid crashing down into the ocean and breaking the suffocating silence that hums through the boardwalk. And there is a silence. Not the kind of silence indicated by absence of sound, as there is still the push and pull of the slow waves of the water, the lazy creak of a wind vane, and the ever present whispers from the markings that brand the walls of the boardwalk's shops and restaurants. It is anticipation. It is an entire town holding its own breath. It is silence that is always here at this time of the night.

Then, there is a disruption in the ocean. The water ripples. There is no longer a silence.

⊰⊱

Jasika has lived in the beach town of Arpenteur for about a month. She went there, as many young artists do, because she doesn't feel that college is the right decision for her, and she isn't wrong about that. However, she has the problem that many millennials face. She doesn't want to put pressure on her parents, who she loves very much, but she can't quite support herself at the age of twenty with nothing on her resume outside of food service and call center jobs. She can't afford to live in one of those cool hipster towns where being a street artist comes with good pay instead of the assumption that she is some sort of vandal. Of course, Jasika has only been a vandal once or twice, but these were strictly confined to severe moments of teenage passion, such as when she spray painted the words "MORT SUX BALLZ" in neon colors on the south wall of her high school when Principal Mortimer suspended off-campus lunch privileges.

In any case, Arpenteur is a perfect town for her. It is a town that prides itself on its diversity. Dozens of different shops make up the little postcard of a boardwalk, everything from an art deco museum straight from *Metropolis* to a Moroccan antique shop worthy of Tangiers. There is a theater where local plays marquee just as much as Tennessee Williams and Arthur Miller. There is a large, freeform garden space, open to whomever wishes to plant something and where the soil never needs to rest. And the food—God, the food—there's just about everything. Cajun, Mediterranean, Japanese eateries sitting alongside good ol' American-style barbecue, pizzerias, ice cream parlors. One would assume the restaurant row of Arpenteur would be an indescribable mix of nasal overload, but it isn't. The smell of it all, it is a meal itself, it is *layered*, the individual scents stacking on top of each other and swirling in your nose without overstaying its welcome. All over the cacophonous sound of romping music, of many energetic languages, of sizzling ovens, of clanging pots, of barking dogs.

You might point out that this place seems to be *exactly* one of those cool hipster towns that Jasika cannot afford to live at. Well, if you look closely at any of the establishments occupying Arpenteur, you will likely find a line of markings in a language you don't know, facing the ocean. These markings first showed up about five years ago in Arpenteur, when it was a much more humble beach town, more of a fishing village than an artistic paradise. These markings came to be known as the Scrawl, and it plays an important part in Arpenteur. Yet, there are only three things known about the Scrawl. The Scrawl is here. The Scrawl provides. The Scrawl does not forgive.

"Look at this," Nazr says with a tone of amused disbelief, sauntering across the boardwalk up to Jasika. Dressed in a pastel button-down with bright red watermelon slices on it, dark hair gelled up, beard trimmed, he looks like a younger Taika Waititi. The smells of the restaurants follow Nazr. One minute it is fresh sourdough bread, then melted queso over a handmade enchilada, then the spices being sprinkled on a golden curry, then crushed grapes distilling in a barrel. Nazr presents his brownie fudge sundae. "They just stuck the brownie on top of the ice cream, like here ya freakin' go, screw off."

"Oh, man, that's no good. Who puts the brownie on top? That's gotta be *drenched* in ice cream."

"Yeah, you get it. Whatever, this will taste amazing anyway." Nazr takes a picture of the sundae on his phone. "What's a good hashtag for this? Hashtag dairy disaster?"

"I like the alliteration, but it's a little negative, and you don't actually seem that mad about it. Maybe something less outraged and more teasing?"

"You right, you right. How about hashtag womp womp? Y'know, like *womp womp*." Nazr sings out the words like a derisive trombone.

"I think that's better."

"Okay here's the full post: Not even small mistakes like this stop me from eating at the Cathy's Creamery! Hashtag womp womp, hashtag Arpenteur life."

"Maybe save the Arpenteur life for like a sunset or something."

"Ah, that's a good plan. Okay, hashtag good vibes it is, then." He posts it, no filter, as always. "This is why I hang around you, Jasika, you make my job easy. So, today's the day, huh?"

Nazr indicates the large rectangle covered in an opaque sheet, attached to a dolly that Jasika has been pulling around the busy boardwalk towards the town hall. She figured taking it through the restaurant row would be the quickest, but now regrets it as hundreds of townsfolk swirl around her like water.

"Yep."

"You nervous?"

"A little."

"Ahh, you'll be fine," Nazr beams. "Graffiti art is like, such a perfect fit for this town. I'm sure they'll love it. Can I do a quick video with you?"

"Ehhh, I'd be more comfortable with just a selfie."

"I can work with that, I can work with that."

They take a selfie that is bright and happy, even with the rather drab-looking rectangle in the background.

"Anything you want me to say about you?" Nazr asks.

"Nah, do what you want."

"Okay, how's this: Good luck, Jasika! I love to see new talent at Arpenteur! Hashtag Passage Day."

Jasika smiles. "Yeah, that sounds good."

Nazr posts it, no filter.

෨෨

The sights of the town, really, the *design* of the town, is like a theme park. There is always something interesting to see or do right in front of you, and some towering monument or glittering lighthouse in the distance, melting time away for any tourist exploring this jambalaya of pleasantness, this sacred lotus of a town.

The town hall is not that impressive, but at the same time is impressive. It's unimpressive in a way that means it is not ornate, it is not gaudy, and it is not particularly new. But there is a strange coolness to it, like an old man who knows how to dress well, or a handmade wooden chair. Simple. Strong. Vaguely intimidating. Lots of dust.

It's a stark contrast to the vibrant glow of the boardwalk. Perhaps the council spent too much time keeping the town that way, making it difficult to make time for renovating their own roost.

Jasika gets approval to enter the council chambers. The wheels of the dolly make a deep rumble against the marble floor, creating an echo through the high-ceilinged room. The seven members of the city council, including Mayor Phil Collins (not that Phil Collins), who Jasika had met on her first day in Arpenteur, all sit in a row behind one of those long podiums that you see in council chambers. All the members have that same strange coolness as the rest of the building. They all wear suits. Startlingly, they are all white. Maybe she should have worn something more subdued instead of her thin button-down with the stained glass window design and the pure white denim jeans. Maybe she should have put her curly hair up instead of letting it sort of poof out like she likes. It is an understatement to say that in a town that seems to be completely at odds with the very idea of homogeneity, the cookie-cutter quality of the council is unexpected.

"Jasika!" exclaims Mayor Phil Collins. "I've been looking forward to this one." Indeed, Mayor Phil Collins had expressed great enthusiasm when he first met Jasika in regards to her plan to present graffiti art.

"Thank you, sir."

"Well, there's not a whole lot of precursor to this. You've already signed up, you're here on time, we're all good on our end. Show us what you got!"

There is a silence of anticipation. Jasika inhales. She pulls the sheet off her piece. She knows it's not her best work. The proportions of the woman are a tad off. The paint has smeared in a few places. She had hemmed and hawed about whether or not to make the font of the words "CHILL OUT" frigid or wispy. She had decided on frigid, but now felt wispy would have been better. But she is proud of the large pink bubble gum bubble inflating from the woman's lips; she had never made something look so perfectly round before. And in this room, where the colors are dull, almost desaturated, the painting is dazzling. Striking.

There is a silence of anticipation.

"Oh, *wow*," gushes Mayor Phil Collins. "I love it!"

There is now praise washing over Jasika from the rest of the council. "So fun, so *casual!*" "The way the blues and greens mesh together, you'd think they would clash, but they don't!" "Love those big earphones, so vintage!" "The peace sign is a cute touch!" "That bubble gum bubble is really damn round!"

Pride wells up in her chest and makes her blush.

⊰৯৯⊱

"Damn, girl!" Nazr gawks at the painting, now hanging prominently in the square in what is essentially the entrance of the town, dedicated entirely to the work of new artists. It will hang here for a month or two until Jasika leaves her mark around town with more pieces. "I'm getting some Jet Set Radio vibes from this! Makes me want to dance just looking at it! Like I should be listening to some lo-fi hip hop beats and skateboarding or whatever."

"Thanks, Nazr."

"Ahh, you *gotta* let me do a video for this. I'll do it on Snapchat, so if you don't like it, it'll be gone in a day, no pressure."

Jasika smiles in spite of herself. "All right, I *guess*."

"Hell yeah!" Nazr gets his phone ready the way an archer might draw a bow. "All you gotta do is, I'll like introduce you, and you just gotta say 'hi' or 'hey guys' or whatever. I'll do the rest."

39

"Okay."

Nazr begins recording. "Hey, what's up y'all, I'm here with my good friend Jasika, there she is."

"Heyyy!" Jasika immediately feels self-conscious. Despite her enjoyment of expressing herself, she never felt particularly comfortable in front of a camera. People like Nazr, who is staying in Arpenteur just on the foundation of his online presence and personality, are a different breed.

"And she just got through her Passage Day with this, like, *really dope* graffiti art. She's gonna be painting the town red, green, and everything in between now, so come on down to Arpenteur and check her stuff out. Later, babes." He stops the recording, and looks at Jasika. "Awesome, awesome. What hashtag do you think goes with this?"

It has been a long day, and Jasika is glad to be back at her studio-slash-apartment. Not a studio apartment, but literally a space that functions as both an art studio and apartment. Really it is a house, but the bedroom part of it was so small it made sense to call it an apartment. It feels empty without the painting she had toiled over since she'd got there, but in some ways feels like the beginning of a new era for her, one where her art is valued a great deal. She will never run out of inspiration in a town such as this. Her studio will open as a real business tomorrow. She calls her parents. They are happy for her. They miss her. She misses them back. She lounges in her chair. She basks in her silence. Her phone rings. It's Mayor Phil Collins.

"Sorry to bother you, I know it's a little late."

"That's okay, sir. What can I do for you?"

"Did you check for the Scrawl? Just wanted to make sure it cleared."

"Oh, right!" In the relief of being done with Passage Day, Jasika completely forgot to look for the markings that were supposed to appear on her building once her work was approved. "No, I haven't."

"That's okay, that's fine. Should be on the west side, facing the ocean."

Jasika steps out of the apartment. The sun was setting. From this angle it looks like the ocean is engulfing it, extinguishing it. The boardwalk crowds are thinning, the town quieting, as it typically does around this time. Jasika checks the west wall of her building. Sure enough, the matte onyx markings she has come to recognize around Arpenteur now occupy a spot on the white wood.

"It's there, yeah."

"Okay, good, great. Yeah, just wanted to check."

"No problem."

"And those markings will probably glow tonight, but that's normal. I promise."

"Right, you mentioned that," Jasika paused. "So that's really it, then? I'm all set?"

"Yes! The Scrawl provides. And again, Jasika, congratulations," Mayor Phil Collins' tone is sincere. "We're really proud to help provide a voice for young, passionate artists such as you. Truly."

"I'm happy to be here."

The call ends. Jasika considers the Scrawl. She thinks of the firstborn sons of Egypt, and of bloodstained thresholds.

⊷⟐⟐⊶

A month later, Jasika's art studio, which she has ironically named "Janksy", is doing well. Her bubblegum pop style of street art is popular among both tourists and residents of Arpenteur. Small canvas paintings are good for a souvenir. More distinguished curators or coffee shop owners are happy to receive larger pieces to spruce up the atmosphere of their homes and places of business. She even has a few wall murals going in places around the boardwalk, including the east side of the town hall.

All for free, of course. Visitors to Arpenteur pay a reasonable price for complete access to the towns' many sights and smells; this money apparently goes towards extraneous expenses, and the Scrawl provides the rest.

Jasika thinks of the Scrawl, and the bone-white glow that beams outside her west side window at night, the thunderous sound of what seems like church organs, and the paralyzing thoughts that needle into her mind in a way that makes it unclear if they are her own thoughts. *Do not go outside. Do not go outside. Keep*

41

working. She shakes away the thoughts. She is here. She is doing what she loves.

Nazr is a regular guest at the studio, whether it is in person for a takeout lunch or in vlog form, telling her (and some six thousand devoted subscribers) of his day in Arpenteur, whether he's unboxing some new tech toy, wakeboarding, or trying some new shawarma or pasta dish or a doughnut with something savory like potato chips on it. Mayor Phil Collins also visits occasionally, as he visits everyone occasionally, monitoring the output and speaking of the Scrawl. Nothing new, but speaking of it nonetheless.

Two more months go by. Business grows exponentially. Jasika now puts out some 25 to 30 paintings a day. It is tiring, but it is still rewarding. The town hall mural is almost complete. The boardwalk acquires more and more of her paintings around the shops. Every day she is delivered more paint. More canvas. More tools. The Scrawl provides.

Two more months go by. Business plateaus. Demand stays high. Jasika is exhausted. The town hall mural remains unfinished. She cannot bring herself to do it this week. Mayor Phil Collins is concerned. The scaffolding that has been on the town hall is kind of an eyesore. He expresses hope that Jasika gets well soon. Every night, bone-white glow.

Jasika has now worked 270 days in a row. Jasika has painted over 7,000 paintings of various sizes and complexities, and around 40 wall murals for other businesses. Her hands shake. Her vision blurs. The art gets sloppy. The art gets boring. Her sentences get monotonous. Her motivation is not there. She has had enough. She has had enough. She decides to close the store tomorrow. Maybe the next day, too. Tonight, bone-white glow.

～§～

Jasika awakes to an empty studio. Not empty of things, and not a depressing emptiness of feeling either. It's an emptiness of paralysis. Shock. Jasika feels as if her studio has been ransacked. As if she has been robbed. She doesn't eat. She curls up on her couch and listens to music that is supposed to help her relax, but it's like oil and water. The music washes over her but doesn't sink in. Eventually she decides it will just stress her out more.

The day goes on. There is a knock at the door. It's Mayor Phil Collins.

"Jasika!" His usual jolliness has been replaced by a plastic, strained jolliness. "May I come in?"

They talk a while over coffee. It's four in the afternoon, but this makes little difference, as Jasika has been relying on caffeine to function. Today, however, it does little to return her to normalcy.

"So no painting today, then?" Mayor Phil Collins gives that same strange, nervous smile. His eyes plead.

Jasika looks down. In this moment, she hates herself. But she must put her foot down.

"I know I might disappoint some people, but I am simply burnt out, sir. Any painting I paint, it won't be good. The passion, it's not there right now. I need some time."

He blinks a few times. His eyes dim a little. "I see. Nothing to be done about it, I suppose."

He stands. "We are proud to be host of such passionate voices such as yourself, all the same. I should be going. You get some rest, Jasika."

He leaves.

⤚⤙

Nighttime. Jasika gets another visitor in Nazr.

"Hey, I heard you were down today. It's been real busy today, but I wanted to check in. I brought a pizza."

It's good to see him. They eat pizza and discuss the finer points of said pizza.

"I thought the whole thing about pizza is that it's like sex?" Nazr says. "Like even if it's bad it's still okay, right?"

"I have a feeling you know little about either pizza or sex," teases Jasika. "Of *course* you can have bad pizza. And bad sex."

"Okay, I mean, yeah, this pizza is trash food, but it's not like, *bad.*"

"No, this is good trash. *Bad* pizza is pizza that tries to be fancy but fails. Y'know what I mean? Like as soon as a pizza *aspires* to be something more, that's when I want it done *right.* I want hand-tossed dough and like, real fresh mozzarella. If they're gonna charge like fourteen dollars for a pizza it better be right!"

"Okay, okay, I gotcha." Nazr laughs a little. "Does that same logic apply to bad sex? Is there also a tier system to like trash-but-good sex and bad-fancy sex?"

They laugh a while. It feels good. Then silence for a while. It's a good silence. Nazr looks around the studio. A feeling of concern injects into the room as the space between whatever he wants to say next lasts a little too long. Tension claws at Jasika's shoulders.

"So," Nazr pauses, the way someone pauses when they consider saying something risky. "Are you gonna be okay?"

Jasika doesn't answer immediately, and every second she doesn't answer the silence grows heavier above them like a rain cloud.

"Yeah, of course. I just need a few days. I'll be back to work soon."

"Okay. That's good." He seems to become fascinated with the last slice of pizza. It has gotten that congealed look pizza gets after a while. "I get it, you know. It gets hard."

"Yeah."

"You get tunnel vision. With me it's always a battle between keeping my people happy, and," he clears his throat. "And, y'know, myself. Keeping myself happy, I mean."

He continues. "I love what I do, really. All these people love me. And I know what it is about me that they love. My positivity. My, like, zest for life, I guess. I live in a cool place. There's always something to take a picture of. People have told me I get them through dark times. And it gets to this point where I have to constantly create, and constantly fight between what belongs to them and what just belongs to me. My whole life right now, I have to decide if I should show things to the world or keep it for myself. And every time I decide to live a moment for me, I feel selfish, y'know? Even now. None of my fans know I'm hanging out with you. And they don't need to. There's a hundred reasons why they don't need to. But I feel selfish, somehow. Because I'm not doing my job when I could be."

Nazr looks frozen as he's talking. Like he's struggling to get every word out. Jasika realizes he's fighting back tears. He looks at her.

"You gotta find that balance, Jasika. It's hard, but you gotta keep hold of yourself. Otherwise you'll just go crazy."

"I know, Nazr. Believe me, I've been doing this too. And yeah. I feel terrible about not producing anything today. But we need the breaks. If you don't do that, then what we love, what we've fought hard to achieve, it's not worth it. It all just..."

She waves her hand. They sit quietly for a while. Nazr sniffs.

"Yeah." He exhales out a guffaw. "Sorry. I didn't mean to like, dump on you, I hope it didn't seem like I was telling you how to live your life or whatever. I guess that was actually more for me."

"It's okay, buddy. We're going to be okay. Okay?"

"Yeah."

There is another silence. This time it's therapeutic.

"Well it's getting late," says Jasika. "I should be going to bed. No sense in saying I need rest if I don't actually do it."

"You right, you right," Nazr sighs. "I'll see you around."

"Totally."

⋞⋟

A bone-white glow roars, bleeding through the window. Jasika wakes with a yelp. Her mind is boiling. Her rooms spins. She smells ozone. She hears church organs. Thoughts pierce into her mind like a tsunami, waves of something that is not her own voice crashing and overlapping and swirling. Her body moves independently from her mind. She tries to scream. Instead she exits her studio.

Outside, Arpenteur is bathed in white light from all the buildings on the boardwalk. Jasika imagines all the faces she's come to know cowering under their sheets as she would do this time of night. From everywhere the Scrawl is comes the haunted organs and blinding light. She walks to the center of the street, her movement jerky, like a toy soldier. She walks down the boardwalk, and it has never felt so long, so stretched before. Arpenteur is moving, it is shaking, Jasika cannot tell if it is a trick of the light, if she is going insane, or if this is actually happening, the shops and the restaurants and the lounges all shifting and vibrating while still leaving a clear path towards the end, towards the water.

She moves toward the beach, mind spinning like an overheated hacksaw. At the end of the boardwalk, above the water, the moon hangs. It's so bright; it looks like it is burning. She

45

shuffles along, past town hall. The water ripples, and something emerges. It is the size of a cruise ship. It is shaped like a seed, or a diamond. It is pure black with bright white markings that zoom around in straight, rigid diagonals across it. This must be it. This must be the Scrawl, somehow, right? Jasika doesn't understand it. Her thoughts are too muddled. It feels like her mind has split. She keeps walking towards it. It hovers in the air, perfectly still, impossibly still, like a glitch. She is at the edge of the pier now. What is probably a few feet across the water feels like miles. Arpenteur seems so far back, the Scrawl so present, the night above it so massive.

Suddenly, all the thoughts in her mind settle into one. There is one voice. It does not sound like any voice you or Jasika or anyone else has heard. If a car crash made words, it would sound more pleasant. If atom bombs spoke a language, it would sound more soothing. If supernovas left behind script after consuming a solar system, it would be easier to understand. This is the voice of the Scrawl.

We are here. We provide. We do not forgive. We are many. We are one. It is this that makes us holy. You have forsaken what is holy.

Perhaps she is in shock, perhaps the cool fire in her that had seemed to fizzle out completely has found a new spark. Perhaps she is truly insane. But Jasika does not feel fear. She feels anger. Deep anger. A broiling, thundering anger that could dry up an ocean. She stares at the Scrawl, this huge obsidian seed.

"I needed a break."

The white markings spinning around the Scrawl move up and down furiously. The Scrawl splits like a cocoon, the shining black carapace lifting off of itself, connected at the very top. Inside, hanging from the center of the top, is a large milky eye with one deep black pupil. It is ablaze with greed and hunger and hatred. Limbs like the legs of a beetle hang from the bottom of the eye like moss.

You are ungrateful. We have given you a gift. We have given everything here a gift.

The limbs lift as if to indicate the boardwalk town of Arpenteur. The whole eye of the Scrawl turns white. The church organs send a wave that knocks Jasika on her back. There is white light everywhere.

We are grateful. We are an individual. We are several. We are final. We are here. We provide. We do not forgive.

And there is a silence. Not a silence as in the absence of sound, for there is still the organs buffeting the boardwalk town, the waves crashing against the pier, Jasika getting off her feet and standing, facing the Scrawl. This thing, this oceanic skin tag of an eyeball monster, will have to try harder than that. Her thoughts erupt against the Scrawl, demanding room. The hideous needles of its voice bend and break in the synapses of her blazing mind.

"Fuck off."

There is a disruption in the sky. There is no longer a silence.

Untitled

Your skin is so soft;
The color almost perfect,
Not too dull or bright.
The lines so faint, barely visible.

I long to touch your face,
To stroke your cheek as
I plunge my knife into your eye,
Carving and scooping your insides out.

The Hook

Tattered skin and ripping leather.
Yellowing meat and congealed blood.
Two hands sewing each other together,
Dirty stains rubbing the mud.
A single wooden hook
Descends, oscillating,
Yearning, reaching for a piece of flesh.
Something to touch,
To feel, to caress,
To puncture, to pierce,
To corrupt, to duress.
Like a living tool it traverses
Through carnal worlds.
It releases the floodgates of ecstasy and earthly desire,
For a reverence of transcendency,
It hooks, connecting
The spirit to the material.
The line, the rope,
Stretches from the sky to the water below,
Tying a noose around the earth,
A safety net for those that know how to use it.
The Hook.

Fleshcrafting, the hook stretches its medium,
Like a good plot it thickens.
It not only grabs your attention,
But punctures it,
Hooking and dragging it.
It dips into the water of life,
Attracting sea creatures of all kinds.
The flesh of centuries hanging off of its wooden sides,
Like honey, dripping,
Brahma, mana, hunangsfall;

The river of life that flows through all;
The sweet, timeless wine.
This swinging hook lays in waiting,
One amongst thousands of rigid infrastructures,
Building the web of the great spider.
Each barb has penetrated the skin of the universe
Playing its own part in this cosmos.

Pull the Petals

His head opened like a wildflower. Each yellowed waxy petal sagging under a ripe wet weight. In the center of these ragged flaps was a shocked pink seed pod broken into shards, peppered by black pellets like the stamen of a trout lily. It smelled of skunk cabbage; sour heat exuding from thick veins, torn loose by sudden and violent force. Vital nectar spilled over its stem and coated the ground with its intoxicating vigor. Flies flocked to the red honey and mired themselves in its full-bodied flavor.

Then came dogs, lapping leaves and breathing hot, mouths snapping dragons. Packs putting petals to their tongues until they melted back to meat. Weathered and worn, the remains were planted in black bags; zipped and shipped away. Presented to the coroner while the garden was kept by the usual groundskeepers. Plucked and pruned by police who made much of every detail in the dirt. The dogs were rounded up and examined as well, put in kennels, some killed. Cadavers for examination.

Squealing wheeling carts heavy and rumbling with split bloodless bodies. Dusty tomes cracked at the right page. The place of pulp and vellum, the end for means to achieve. Plucking pits from these husks; filed and organized like a well-kept shed of spades. Placed in wrappers, crinkling seeds scattered to mindful loam. Growing new thoughts.

Thistle theories catching at my hocks. Roots writhing into my molded clay. By sawing into old timber, I have spawned saplings; splitting the canopy and shedding its light into the needling forest floor. How many more might spring from that ground? Those green stems hurtling skyward under the suns interrogating rays.

No. I will shuck the thorns from the stem and set them severed in a vase. I will pull the petals one by one. Which ears of corn have bent to my sound, what wiry grapevines swell with the fruit of my labor? I will salt the earth and sow them in the acid ground where no life grows. Clawing for footholds among the stones and finding none they will scatter to the winds. I will reap what I have sown.

There were three.

The first, a farmer at market on the fated day. Found in the fields of his own homestead, hands hidden in the dirt. If only he could've kept his own garden. I set steel teeth on his footpath. He shuffled, sandaled feet feeling out the first bite, before falling upon the lethal crop. Neck snapped on the iron spring fox-trap, his head hanging slack just beyond the jaws. The time-tanned bald spot at his crown rounded by retreating white hair reminded me of a Venus flytrap's flower. I took a plastic bag full of vegetables when I left.

The second drove a semi and spat tobacco like a snake. Chewing on cured leaves as if cud for cattle. He was holed up in a hotel; I heard him hacking up a lung from the bottom floor. He snored horribly when I stole into the hostel at night. I walked a barrel of acid up the stairs before dragging him into the tub to drain it. Piranha solution stewed him in the belly of that Cobra lily while I stole soap and pillow-covers at his expense.

The third, a wonderful woman by all accounts, had a very modern house. Big billowing curtains played like the one long white wing of peace lilies. They wrapped around, gasping for air with her as she threw the window open. Gas filtered from the room while I walked away, curtains in tow.

That was how they found me, flashing rich reds and eye-blinking blue. A dirty truck full of rotting vegetables, stolen soap, pillow-covers, toga wrapped in curtains. The trial was as fast as a bamboo shoot. Guilty, I was sentenced to death.

They put me in a wooden planter. I hung from the neck, white, pink, then red like a begonia.

Becoming Prayers

O, how those Stigmata slaughter, marking cuts
in those pagan backforms with rakeleather;
cast oracle stones,
twinkling legends of Urania's mirror,
the clickity-clack, clickity-clack of
Our recumbent bones
like petrified flutes strung in natural wells.
primrose paths we walk upon, fretting on the
pink-red tones.

Whistling within that stone wind;
thrashing / slashing / thrashing / slashing
Our palms! Our psalms! O hollow! O hallow!
Whistling to that leaking blood foam.

but what is this change in air?
this taut feeling—this hanging feeling?
this held feeling—this O O O delight?
O iris? O sclera? O snapped milk thistle?
but what if it was the chrysanthemums?
they that dangle in a yellow impiety,
that whiten and whiten and whiten
in knuckles of bliss?
in shirts of hair; Nessus' robe; our cilice?
Our eyes, O, Our eyes!
Our imperfect indulgence.
O, our disenchanting anathema:

        How
with each——————lash;——————We whistle.
        How
with each——————gash;——————We smile.

We are moon food and Venus is looking down at us in hysterics as she holds her scales, bullheaded, balancing her heels and the crooks of her arches on the blade of a labrys

I've never stood a mere few feet away from a sputtering caldera,
never ran into a literal burning building to save a dead thing
thinking maybe, just maybe.

But I did get used to the thought of having your eyes to look at for
    the rest of my life.
I imagine the burn is something like that—
like picturing actually living to be 80 years old for the first time,
having a second signature on forms to foster kids,
thinking my family would *get it* if they could just see what her
    eyes would do to me when the vows began and the veil was
    lifted.

But then never finding the words to describe the shape of your
    eyes,
or their tender intensity with a tendency to rip away any sense of
    footing I thought I had.
Because instead, I saw the last flicker of faith I had in you go out,
smelled the salt and soot in the air,
when our dearest malefic Mars traveled east and west,
leading us to see what little we had worth fighting for.

You, with the moon in its fall,
my faith was a log cabin I built to weather the winter of you that I
    anticipated,
but not the one that came.
I could have never known your love required things like gloves
    indoors—
where I thought I'd be guaranteed warmth—
until I looked at the sopping wet ashes myself;
the ones left by every fight ignited with no true end in sight.

For this reason,
I am indebted to mars, retrograde as she was.
As she will be again.
A tentative, honey, dust-covered cremation chamber
for not letting me keep running into a home both avalanche and
    forest fire;
for keeping me from believing I ever have to
or could
be
"warm enough for the both of us."

Renata

She is young and vibrant, pulsing with life to the point of overflow. Her messy red hair is pulled into a bun that does little to control the frizzy locks. The bridge of her nose is a touch too wide, her eyes a bit too far apart. Her fair skin is accentuated by a multitude of freckles, as if they have been splashed upon her face in a moment of chaotic randomness. Her jean shorts are worn, with ragged edges. Her shoes are scuffed, the soles falling apart. Her pink shirt reads "Tea Rex" and is accompanied by a graphic of a large reptile wearing a monocle, top hat, and fake mustache, holding a cup of tea in its claws. He finds the pink shade unflattering, believes that it clashes with the fire of her hair. Nor does he appreciate the humor behind the graphic, his eyes narrowed as he sorts through every name he can recall that has been attributed to the caricature on her shirt.

He cannot help but wonder what message she is trying to convey.

He gives up, crediting his failure to human fashion, which changes so often he does not try to keep abreast of it. He wears black suits because they are simple; the whims of fashion are beyond him.

She wears a nametag on her shirt. It is white with the words "HELLO MY NAME IS" printed in bright red ink. "Renata" is written in the box below, every letter perfectly structured; every ink stroke intentional. He does not recognize the name she chose, but he feels the intent behind it. Words are power and names even more so. He knows her true name: the one that was once whispered in prayers and dedications and echoed in the stone halls of holy temples.

It echoes now through the depths of his soul, beats through the chambers of his ancient heart. He is the only one who remembers.

She shifts in her chair as she adjusts her position, tucking her bare legs underneath her and exposing her clothed form in the most delicious way. His eyes drink in the curve of her body. With every breath she takes her breasts tremble, her shoulders rise and fall. The scent of vanilla drifts from her in gentle waves like the sea lapping at the shore. Motes of dust dance upon the pale flesh of her thighs, inviting him to touch her. To feel her in a way that he has not for centuries.

He realizes he is staring and turns his head away, berating himself for violating her modesty.

Beeping interrupts his thoughts, reminds him of why he is here. With little effort, his gaze shifts from the woman sitting cross-legged in her chair to the occupant of the hospital bed. The contraption she is attached to continues to wail, warning everyone within range that something has gone wrong. Dark, tired eyes glance at the IV bag. Renata leans forward and pushes buttons without any sort of caution.

The beeping stops, and a blessed silence descends upon the hospital room.

The peace is broken by a haggard nurse bustling through the doors with a self-important air and the hunched shoulders of one who is exhausted by the weight of the world. She brushes past him, nudging him with her sharp elbows but does not apologize. Nor does he expect one. She cannot, after all, see him.

Nicotine encases her in a thin film, the acrid smell burning his nostrils and cutting through the sterile air of the hospital. He knows she has cancer, can sense it eating away at her lungs; it is merely a matter of time before he hears her bells.

"I turned it off," Renata explains to the nurse, her soft voice filling the room with warmth. "We didn't know how long it'd be before anyone could get around to this part of the ward."

The nurse harrumphs, looking down her nose at Renata before double-checking the machine and fussing about with the machinery. "Young lady, I've told you before, don't touch the equipment." Her voice is harsh, and it is grating upon his ear. He does not wish to hear it again.

"You are the only one who complains."

"Do it again and I'll ask you to leave."

"Didn't you say that last time?"

The nurse glares at her and receives a bright smile for her troubles. She ignores Renata after that, exchanging the wilted IV bag for a plump one full of clear liquid. She gives Renata one last glare before she walks away, her white sneakers squeaking on the linoleum floor.

Renata pulls a face, scrunching her nose and sticking her pink tongue out at the nurse's retreating back before winking at the old woman in the bed. The woman lets out a weak laugh, her tired eyes twinkling with mischief. She squeezes Renata's hand with her own withered appendage, clinging to the very fabric of life as if afraid to let go.

He briefly wonders what Renata's hand would feel like in his.

The entire universe, everything that is, was, and ever will be, held in the palm of his hand.

A tremor runs down his spine.

The tinkling of a thousand bells echoes through his mind. He turns away from the scene before him, looking into the past, the present, the future. He is everywhere and nowhere at once. He is here in this moment and flung throughout the whole of the universe. Wherever there is life, he comes to take it away.

He haunts battlefields that are rife with the smell of death and the moans of the dying: the valleys of Sumer blend with the hills of Italy, Hadrian's Wall, the American plains. He cradles a baby in his arms as the mother clings to an empty shell, pleading with gods long dead for the return of her child. He lurks in the shadows as prostitutes are murdered in the streets of London. He watches the towers fall. He witnesses the last act of a desperate man.

He walks amongst the stars, calling lost remnants of humanity home.

She is there, always in the peripheral of his vision. Her form is never the same, shifting into an aspect of life that allows for the acceptance and understanding of mortals. He knows her all the same; feels her aura pulsing and vibrating and churning beneath the mortal mask she wears. She is turned away, silhouetted against an English sunset, the moon's pale reflection upon the ocean, a flickering oil lamp.

She will not witness the moment life passes into his domain.

This is their cosmic dance. They are destined to remain in this state, weaving in and out of each other's eternal existence. He longs to tell her to forsake the dance and to join with him for a final time. He is tired and ready for the end of all things to come; the moment the universe collapses on itself and all life slips into the endless dream.

Once more, the tinkling of a thousand bells calls to him. As he turns away she begins to shift her fiery gaze upon him. He longs to return that fire. He wants to whisper her true name in her ear, and to hear his own in return, her breathy voice laced with lust and devotion.

Fear and desire war within him as he moves away, turning back to the scene in the hospital room. The woman's grip upon Renata's hand has lessened. Her withered chest shudders with quick, panicked breaths, and her eyes wildly search the room.

She cries out when she sees him, staring into the depths of his soul and unable to look away. He sees his own exhaustion reflected in the old woman's eyes, and he knows she is ready.

"Come, Evelyn," he calls to her in his gentle voice, holding out a hand. "Allow me to take you home. Your family is waiting for you."

Renata is looking at him now, drawn to the sound of eternity that reverberates in his speech. He expects her to turn away from this moment as she has, does, will with so many others. She catches him off guard by staring into his eyes, waiting. Watching.

Evelyn drops Renata's hand and reaches out, her fear melting away and in its place relief that her journey is finally over. He meets her halfway, brushing his fingertips against her wrinkled palm, and he witnesses the life she once lay claim to; it is beautiful.

The alarms go off once more, but Evelyn no longer cares.

He stands guard over the body she has abandoned, watching as the haggard nurse arrives, bringing with her a rush of activity as humanity continues to move ever onward.

Renata stands next to him. She is so close to him that if he chooses to, he can reach out and brush her fingertips with his own. He resists the temptation, though it is a very near thing.

"Why are you here?" He knows the answer to this question. He has asked it of her on other occasions and will do so again, he is sure. It is part of the dance. That is what he tells himself.

The truth is that he simply needs to hear her say the words that always come.

"I am always here." She gestures at their surroundings as she speaks, and he knows she refers to the chaotic hustle and bustle of mortal life. He tries to smile at her and fails, feeling brittle and worn.

She surprises him by shifting the tone of this eternal game they play. "I came because I was needed."

"They will always need you. You give them hope."

"No," she responds softly. "You needed me."

Before he can inquire about the meaning of her words, she reaches out, brushing away the tear he shed for the life of Evelyn. She stares at the teardrop that now rests on the tip of her finger, but he only sees her. His flesh burns where she touched him. He searches through the myriad of mortal languages he knows, but there are no words capable of conveying the intensity of his feelings for her. All the platitudes that begin to form shrivel into nothing before falling from his lips, leaving him feeling lost and frustrated.

Renata looks up at him. Her eyes are beautiful, a green ocean framed by thick black lashes that flutter like the delicate wings of a butterfly. He counts the freckles splattered across her face and knows the constellations they create. He sees the dryness in her skin, the flecks that are beginning to develop on her lower lip. Her pink tongue darts out, and he is mesmerized by the moisture it leaves in its wake.

She returns his intensity with boldness, those eyes taking in his own features with a ferocity of one who knows time is not on their side. Desire falls thick and heavy between them and he longs to feel those chapped lips pressed against his own.

He cannot bring himself to take the next step. Renata is the one to break down the barriers between them. To end and begin their dance again.

"Please," she is saying to him, "come home."

He hesitates but knows he cannot resist her plea. Mortals always assume that he is chasing her, hunting her, consuming her. They never consider, he thinks as he stares into her ancient eyes and grasps the hand held out before him, that it is she who hunts him, seeking not an end, but a beginning.

Rebirth.

Renewal.

Their fingers entwine, the gesture intimate. He feels her squeeze his hand and he smiles, closing his eyes as he revels in the feeling of life that flows through his veins and sets his heart racing.

Death holds the entire cosmos in his hands: everything that is, was, and ever will be.

She is beautiful.

Death of a Succubus

I am attached to your meaning,
    to your being,
        to your worth.

I want to taste your soul;
    to lick the waste of your thoughts
        as you ponder my commitment.

I have no meaning for this,
    these feelings of peace I have,
        the joy I get from you.

I am attached to your being,
    to my meaning,
        to our worth.

No longer do I exist,
    no single being,
        we are attached as one.

My mind is joined with your soul,
    my soul invades your mind;
        you relinquish yourself to me.

Attached, my lips to yours,
    our heart beats as one,
        our thoughts merge.

I exist because of you.
    You reached down and called,
        and I came.

la fin du monde

Parsnips. Celery. Chalk. Glue. Ribbon. Peanut Butter. Steering Fluid.

What could someone possibly need this random assortment of items for? Are they cooking, working on a car, and doing arts and crafts?

"Oh, and a pack of gum."

Which gum? Which of the forty selections of gum does he want? I hand him Juicy Fruit. He hands me a twenty-dollar bill.

"It's $22.40"

"Huh?"

"Your total. It's $22.40. You handed me a twenty."

"Oh."

He hands me a five. I hand him his change.

"Thanks."

Working at Marty's is a stupid experience. Some customers are assholes. Some are—stupid. Some are fake and cloying. Every day I do this, except for Saturday. On Saturday I watch basketball. At least when it's basketball season. If it's not basketball season then I watch football. If it's neither basketball nor football season I sleep and drink. If it *is* basketball or football season I still drink.

On Saturdays I drink.

Chocolate. Pepsi. Frozen Pizza. Scratchy ticket. 10 on 7.

Nobody ever wins off scratchers. Well, I guess some people do. It wouldn't be this person. Nobody that eats buffalo chicken frozen pizza wins anything. It's time for my break. I step outside and check social media. An asteroid. A big asteroid. It's going to hit the earth. In March. At the beginning of March. It's October. That's five months from now. This is a joke. I check the other outlets. This is not a joke.

If they don't figure something out, we're all going to die. I pull the flask out of my pocket. I drain it. If the world ends in March then I'm going to miss March Madness. Everyone is going to miss March Madness. There won't be a March Madness. There won't be a March Madness. There won't be a March. Shit. Butler was really looking good this year. That's their luck, though. Ranked number one, legitimate shot at the title, and the world's going to end before they have the chance to win it.

I look at the sky. I don't see an asteroid. Of course I don't. I realize I'm stupid. It's probably for the best that I die. I check social media again. Hey, Syracuse beat Saint Mary's. Nice. The Spurs are 14 and 1. Looking good. I look at the sky again. Still no asteroid. Should I quit my job? I have six months to live. A good-looking woman walks by. She grabs me and kisses me. I'm disoriented.

"It's the end of the world!"

She slurred her words. Who the fuck is drunk at three in the afternoon on a Tuesday?

She walks off. I'll never see her again. She was good-looking. I put the flask to my lips. It's empty. Oh. I'm drunk at three in the afternoon on a Tuesday. The world's ending, though, so fuck it. I should call my parents. No, I'll wait for them to call me. If they haven't heard yet, I don't want to be the one to tell them. I need to go back to work. I walk back in. Everybody is celebrating. The world is ending. Why is everyone celebrating? It's frozen buffalo chicken pizza guy.

"I won! Twenty thousand dollars!"

First time for everything. I should scratch all the tickets for fun. My phone is ringing. I pick it up. Is it my parents? No. I don't recognize the number. I answer it.

"Roger! Are you okay? The asteroid, Raj, it's bad, your father says…"

Oh. Right. She got a new phone number.

"…and it's the gays, Roger. It's the homosexuals. God is…"

On the news they're saying NASA has been working on a tractor beam, but they aren't hopeful. Apparently last month the beam successfully nudged a nickel two whole millimeters. What a powerhouse of a machine.

"…and you know I don't hate them, Raj, I'm friends with that woman, Cindy, but it's still wrong."

"Mom, I've got to go, love you."

Why do the Protestants always think it's because of gay people?

It's one big gay natural disaster after another with them.

"Roger, we've got a line, bud."

He has an apologetic look on his face.

"I know it's the end of the world and everything, but people still want their shit."

I take off my name badge and set it on the counter. I pick up a bottle of whiskey and take a swig.

"Roger, what are you doing?"

"Every day is Saturday now, Mark."

AUTHOR STATEMENTS

Ode to Tequila and **Death of a Succubus** were written by **Heathermarie Moats**. Heathermarie enjoys a cup of strong tea, cats, and trashy romance novels; however, she absolutely does not enjoy writing. When not writing, she takes pleasure in the randomness of friends, tattoos, and travel; but as a student, she is always writing.

Year Walk was written by **Ryder David Parker**. Ryder says: I've always been a dreamer, too often a day-dreamer, which got me scolded by more than a few teachers and my own parents. But I found a home in the places of my imagination and a good story so I never stopped dreaming.

Spring and **Renata** were written by **Jessica Stephens**. Jessica is a former student of NSU, having graduated with a BA in history and a minor in creative writing, and is a graduate student at OU. She lives in Salina with her three dogs: Peach, Cocoa, and Luna.

Up With the Sun and **On Turkey Mountain** were written by **Daniel Cade Straight**. Daniel, born and raised in Wyoming, is a lifelong writer and hiker. These are his first formally published poems.

An Abject Abstract was written by **E. Llan Pate**. Llan says: Just a small town boy trying to find his place in the world. I believe the phrase "anything is possible" is both a lie in the face of reality and a fact of the imagination.

Twoworlds was written by **Ronny Vann**. Ronny is retired, full-blood Cherokee, a Sequoyah H.S. graduate (1974), a U.S. Army veteran (74-77), and a member of Tahlequah Writers. He started writing church news and letters to the editor, was published in *Green Country Anthology*, and lives in Barber Community.

Mr. Melvin Quit Today was written by **Tyler Maruca**. Tyler is a student at NSU majoring in creative writing.

A Visitor to my Jail was written by **Sarah Usry**. Sarah says: I am an education major and creative writing enthusiast that has been writing novels and composing poems since grade school. Refusing to just be another statistic, poetry and God Almighty have always been my battle armor, to great effect.

Wolves Howl Softly was written by **William "Wile" Barthelemy**. William is an NSU student graduating in Spring 2019 with Bachelor of Arts degrees in Creative Writing and English.

The poem beginning **"Hungry children laugh"** was written by **Mary Hanafee**. Mary is a free spirit, connoisseur of life, and vehement arch-nemesis of Someday. She can recite the *Lord of the Rings* movies from memory but can't remember her bank account number. She's waiting for the aliens to come get her.

WM-FX195 was written by **Shuna Verjaska-Hoag**. Shuna is a gay author whose works tend to revolve around their experiences with gender, identity, mental health, and poverty.

Snowglobes was written by **Lakin Aleyse**. Lakin is a 24-year-old Native American writer from Lost City, Oklahoma. She is a Gates Millennium Scholar, former Write Club president, and recent NSU graduate. Lakin writes poetry, short fiction, and what she calls "true crime fiction."

The Boardwalk was written by **Bradley Dame**. Bradley enjoys cold weather and coffee.

The poem beginning **"Your skin is so soft"** was written by **Phebe Lebeaux**. Phebe dreams of residing in a seaside cottage, watching the whitecaps greet the seagulls and sipping wine. When not writing, she enjoys traveling the backroads and stopping to enjoy the company of strangers and local boutiques.

The Hook was written by **Ian "AWੴ" McAlpin**. Ian/AWੴ is a Cherokee Natchez artist and scholar on their way to promoting indigenous language and culture through the arts and archival preservation. An Alum of NSU, Ian is attending the MLIS program at OU, focusing in archive studies.

Pull the Petals was written by **Kyle Stevens**. Kyle is an NSU student studying literature and creative writing.

Becoming Prayers was written by **Zachary Knutson**. Zachary says: I am a first generation student majoring in History Education. I have always enjoyed writing poetry. I like the letter O and the number 8. My two favorite books are *Sirens of Titan* and *Pale Fire* by Nabokov.

We are moon food… was written by **Allison Childress**. Allison is a past Louder Than a Bomb competitor, future history teacher, perpetual bad joke maker, & lesbian (who uses they/them pronouns). They are passionate about reflecting and engaging to build a socially, economically, and politically sustainable and just life.

la fin du monde was written by **Jordan Riddles**. Jordan is a writer of flash fiction and poetry from Poteau, Oklahoma. Most of his writing is inspired by Oklahoma itself, and the people that live there; hoping to carry over something from home in each piece.

A Note on Author Information

text: *the body of a poem, story, or essay*

paratext: *everything else (or, as Philip Lejeune put it, "a fringe of the printed text which in reality controls one's whole reading of the text")*

The Talon's editors have chosen to include author names and biographies in the back of the journal to allow a first reading of the text/s free from the influence of paratextual information.

SUBMISSION GUIDELINES

If you're interested in submitting your writing or art to *The Talon* (and we very much hope that you are!) please read the following guidelines for information about the submission process.

We accept prose and poetry submissions. This year, for the first time, we are also accepting submissions of black-and-white art to be included in the journal. You are welcome to submit work in more than one category. Submissions are open to NSU students, faculty, staff, alumni, and other community members. All submissions must be your own original work.

Prose (Fiction and Creative Nonfiction)
- You may submit up to three pieces of prose per reading period.
- Your *entire* prose submission should be no more than 6,000 words in total.
- Prose should be single-spaced, in 12-point Times New Roman font.
- Please do not include your name on your submission document (but do include it in your email).

Poetry
- You may submit up to five poems per reading period.
- Please begin each poem on a new page.
- You *entire* poetry submission should be no longer than ten pages in total.
- Poems should be single-spaced, in 12-point Times New Roman font.
- Please do not include your name on your submission document (but do include it in your email).

Art

- You may submit up to five black-and-white images per reading period.
- Each image should be at least 300dpi and designed to fit a 6x9 page.

Cover Art

- Please email or check our facebook page for further updates on submitting cover art!

Submissions may be emailed to SubmitToTheTalon@gmail.com. The deadline for submissions for Volume 4 of *The Talon* is September 15, 2019. We're looking forward to seeing your work!

54634784R00050

Made in the USA
Columbia, SC
03 April 2019